The Adventures of James and The Murder Mystery

By Hariram Suthakaran

First Published 20th July 2020

First Edition

Font: American Typewriter

Copyright © 2020

by Hariram Suthakaran

The Adventures of James and the Murder Mystery

ISBN: 9798667899303

To My sister with Love!

Table of Contents

Chapter 1: The Moving

James awoke, thinking about the attack that happened in July.

'I could have died!' he thought to himself.

He got out of bed
and went down to see
his Godfather in a
handsome suit with
black socks with
polished shoes.

"Good, good; you're
awake!" Said
Professor David, who
was making
breakfast.

"Yeah, I just woke up." Replied James

"Alright, pack up your going to be staying at Max's," said Professor David

"Why?" asked James

"Well, I have an important meeting with the leader of superpowers on the return of the villain." Said Professor David

"Ohh, do you where Max lives?" asked James

"Yeah, his mother is a cleaner at the ministry," said Professor David

"Oh okay, I will go and pack." Said James as he left to pack

James did like Max,
but he didn't want to
go to his house since
he never went there
before nor did max
ever come to his
house, but he said
nothing because he
could already see his
Godfather was quite
stressed.

James did not pack
very much because
He and James were
the same age so he
thought he could wear
his clothes.

"James are you
ready?" said
Professor David

"Yes, I'm coming!"
Shouted James

They left feeling
alright and Professor
David felt better as
he was not going to
be late.

Chapter 2: Max's home

When they arrived, James felt anxious but just went with the flow.

They knocked on the, door and James's Mom Mrs. Robin opened the door.

"Oh hello! We were
expecting you a little
late but come on in!"
said Mrs. Robin

"Okay, I will see you
at, school James.
Bye!" said Professor
David

Professor David left
in a hurry. James
stepped inside to see
a magnificent house
with amazing pictures
and a fantastic living
room. The house was
three stairs high and
completely ran
on magic.

"Come on, dear! Have a seat." Said, Mrs. Robin

"Hey, Mum, can you keep it. down I'm-"
"WAIT, you never told me James was going to come!"

"Hey, James. Let me go change and I will come back down."

"Okay, Max." Said, James

During the next month, Max and James had the best of times. Playing with action figures, practicing magic and having amazing breakfast. James had never had so much fun in his whole life in fact he didn't even remember the last

time he had so much
fun

It was until 27th
August they left the
house to go to scrubs
in Mrs. Robin's fancy
car.

It had a high-end
radio that could play
any music and the
windows weren't
actually windows.
James and Max
brought over some
action figures so they
could play in the car.

Even though James didn't really need to go Scrubs since his Godfather had already bought all the things he needed, but he went along with the plan anyway. James went and watched Mrs. Robin and Max as they bought the things they need. Max's family was not very rich so he could only get second-hand items. James hated to see his friends buy worn-out clothes, so he gave them some money

"Thank you so much, James. You know you did not have to do that."

"I had to. I could not stand seeing my best friend wearing worn-out clothes that people could make fun of. I'm not your friend anyway, I'm your brother."

Mrs. Robin started to cry but tried to hide it. They hugged each other and carried shopping.

They bought him a brand-new umbrella that had a electronic shocker that is perfect for attacking people.

They bought a new cape that could actually help him fly (James also bought one) and his books for the year

Once they had bought all their supplies they went back home.

Chapter 3: School is Cancelled

James woke up in Max's room to see no max, but hear a woman crying. He realized it was Mrs. Robin. He dashed downstairs to see Mrs. Robin reading the newspaper. The newspaper was

written by Jackson
Kandy and read;
SCHOOL IS
CANCELLED
On 21st July 2008, a
kidnapping of a little
girl happened. Her
name was Savannah,
she was a Year 2 and
was supposed to be
going into the Year 3.
Now, the leader of

magic has shut down the school of superpowers and we don't think it will be opening for a while. If the girl is not found the leader of magic may open a full investigation. *

For my on this story turn to page 7.

*We, NewsOfWizarding, have no claims this will happen. We are just suspecting.

Written by Jackson Kandy.

James could not
believe his eyes. A
girl was kidnapped.
School was cancelled.
James did not want
to get involved, so all
he did was run
upstairs find max and
tell him. James came
rushing down. He was
so bumped that
school was cancelled

since Year 2 were allowed in the bigger and more spacious playground and he could have started a new class called Noils: Their Life.

James did not know
what to do except
open up his new
textbook and start
studying. Max did the
same thing.

Max learned that
noils have to grow
fruit and can't just
magically grow them
with superpowers.

Hours, Days, weeks went by of this until there was an update in the article.

The Article Read;

She is DEAD! As we all know a girl named Savannah was kidnapped. The investigators have told us she was found dead. She died due to the winter war curse. This curse freezes the person to death. The investigators have

told us there was a
note that read;

Dear whoever reading
this note,
I was told to kill her
by the villain. He
would have killed me
and my son. Please
don't kill me if you
ever find out who I
am.

Signed

OD

We have not been told by the investigators who OD or how he knows The Villain.

Written by Mandy
Goatley

James and Max could
not believe his eyes.
They went and
upstairs and had an
idea that was not
safe, but they had to
do.

"Are you thinking
what I'm thinking?"

"Yep!" said Max

"We are going to save
them!"

James and Max
packed their bags and
jumped out the
window carefully

Chapter 4: School Starts

James and Max stayed at a Hotel near Lambeth Bridge. They got copies of the Superpower News and had an amazing breakfast every day. This was all fun and games until they got a copy of the newspaper.

SCHOOL STARTING; PARENTS GET EXCITED

Leader of Magic told us in an interview that the School of Superpowers is safe to open. The school will take extra precautions and students that don't appear will be immediately apart of a world superhero search.

Article by Lola Sana

James felt like he was going to get sick. He could not believe that the Leader of Magic actually allowed schools to open up again. James went up to max then just turned back because he did not want to tell him.

James and Max left
the hotel and
explored the area
they were in. The
only reason they
came to Lambeth was
because Max did
research and found
out that most
Supervillain kidnapping
happens near
Lambeth. Meanwhile,

Mrs. Robin was calling every single person who worked for The Leader of Magic. Everyone picked up and said they would have a full investigation except Professor David.

James and Max were looking around and found an old abandoned house. They started looking around and decided to make their secret hideout just in case anyone knows their real location. They find a well. It was quite dirty, but they

knew they could
replenish it with a bit
of powers.

"Wato Clean!"
Shouted Max

Max had replenished the room. They both left their secret hide out and went back to the hotel to get their stuff. Mrs. Robin was the world's most stressed person at that moment. She called everyone and then she decided to call the Unite Police,

the highest police in
the Superpower
world.

Meanwhile James and Max were just on their break and were just sitting down; relaxing. Until their daily newspaper came by which the left the two boys in an immediate shock

A newspaper article went out and it read;

ANOTHER GIRL GOES MISSING

A girl named Emilia Wayne goes missing on the 3rd of October. She was last seen playing outside in the garden. Maya, a year 2 this year is very upset.

School once again is closed, according to investigators and the government officials.

Written by Tammy Lingerie

James and Max
immediately contacted
Maya and were sad
on how she was
crying.

They told her their
address and she could
join them on their
mission. She was very
hesitant but agreed.

A couple of days went by and she finally arrived and she brung a copy of that week's newspaper and she recapped what it said.

"Guys listen to this!"

"The government
officials have told all
to stay inside and not
to leave. Those who
do leave could face
serious prosecution
and could be sent to
jail for life. Minors
will not be affected
by this but if your
minors do leave stop
them immediately."

James took a deep
gulp but said nothing.

Meanwhile, Mrs.
Robin read that
article she was
furious that no one
can leave their home,
but she had a plan.

She contacted Mrs.
Wayne, Maya's mum,
and told her
everything from how
the two boys are
gone and much more.

Then Mrs. Wayne told her that her oldest daughter Maya was missing. So, they agreed to meet up and find the kidnapper and their children.

Chapter 5: the best friends disappear

James awoke the next day to see not Max or Maya. There was note next to him that said;

Dear James,
I have your friends max and James. Give me 5,000 nocks.
Signed, OD

At first James
thought OD was a
person who was in a
depression but
actually he was a
mean rotten person
unless someone was
asking for that
money.

He had also just realized he still had the undying necklace, the necklace that could not kill him.

James did not know
what to do without he
is sidekicks, so he
had to improvise. He
used Max's research
machine found out
that the most
Supervillain kidnapping
place had changed to
Coventry. He used
Maya's outfits to
disguise himself as

ministry worker and put high heels to make himself look much taller. He had just left the well when wonkers came and tried to catch James. He used his umbrella and threw snake around one and burnt another one. The others flew away

and James rushed to
Mrs. Robin house
where they had a
chat.

"James, where have
you been? We have
been worried sick."

"Max and Maya are missing. They were kidnapped and could be the next to die."

They two parents started to cry, and they called back up together they all went to their secret hideout.

They investigated
everything from the
mirror to the floor.
They checked the
suitcases and finally
the most important
part of the puzzle
the note. They
immediately called
the superpower
scientists lab.

Just before they
could take it away
sinkers came and took
it. And dropped over
some snakes. They all
fought until the
sinkers capuchin the
upper hand and hit
James in the tummy.
He passed out and
found himself in the
hospital.

James woke up to see two government officials. They told him everything that had happen and said that Mrs. Wayne and Robin had gone to stop them.

James knee he was
not allowed to leave
but he had an extra
bottle of Teleport
medicine. He asked
for a cup water and
as they left, he left
too.

Chapter 6: Where are they?

James had no idea where the two parents were, but he was very dizzy, and his superpowers were all wonky. He stared shooting everything in sight. Breaking glass, making cars run over people and much more.

James was not sure with his plan what he should do. He took another gulp off the teleportation potion and asked it to take him to their secret base.

The base though was
completely horrible.
Al the walls had been
ripped down to find
evidence, his action
figures were all
broken and the
picture of his mum
and dad was burnt.

He started to cry
and wished that
someone would come
and help him. Until he
realized that his
undying necklace was
not invisible but was
shining a really bright
red and green and it
started making him
spin.

Chapter 7: Emilia's Death

James is taken to the future where he stands in a black suit, in front of a grave and the name was Emalia Wayne.

He realized that if he did not stop that person, they would be having a funeral for Emalia and next it could be Max and Maya.

James started crying and saw that right next Emilia Grave was Mrs. Robin.

He dashed to the
exit of the Funeral
and saw that the city
was in runes. He
knew that he might
have to sacrifice
himself to save his
friends and family.

James touched the necklace to take him back to his special fort.

James touched his necklace and asked it to take him to the location of James.

"INVINSON!"
Shouted James to make himself invisible and invincible.

It did not take him anywhere, but it brought two people over.

"MAX, MAYA! WHERE WERE YOU?"

"That dude came
here at night and
came and took us
away. He tortured us
and tried killing us,
but we could not."
Said the two them

"I'm so happy you guys are here, and I think I know why you're not dead."
Said James

"Why?" asked the two

"I learned this in my textbooks. If you have faith that you're going to survive any curse that will kill you, you can't die and there is something I need to tell you.

"My undying necklace turned a really dark red and green, so I touched it. It took me to the future, and I was at Max's mums funeral and Emilia's funeral."

"WHAT! WE HAVE
TO STOP THAT
PERSON." Shouted
the two of them

"James, I have
something to tell you
something. Your
godfather is the
kidnapper."

"It can't be. He told
me that-"

"That he was going to
meet the leader of
magic. We know."
said Max

"I know where is if you are sure that he is the kidnapper. I know his secret hideout come with me."

Chapter 8: He is found

James, Max and
Maya teleport to the
location, where they
find Professor David
about kill Mrs. Robin.

"STOP!" Shouted
James

"Oh, hi James." Said
Professor David

He took out his
umbrella and started
shooting with his
umbrella.

James told Max and
Maya to put they
hand on their heart
and say, come out
please, please come
out.

They did what they were told to do and their protectors started to attack Professor David.

"Stop them James. NOW!" shouted Professor David

"No! You are a criminal. Killing people. I thought you were my father!"

"No, I am. I was being held against will. I'm not lying."

"I don't care. Protectors attack him now!"

He was then
attacked, and he
fainted.

Chapter 9: The Sentence

They were all at court. Waiting for a response from the judge.

James said nothing, so did Max and Maya.

The Judge came in
and Professor David
was locked up in a
chair!

"After hearing the response from many parties, I would have to say Oliver David, you are being sentenced to 25 years in prison. Said the Judge

"I'm sorry Dad, but bye."

"Wait! Before anyone leaves, my son will be taken in custody by Mrs. Jenifer Wayne. I hope they all live a happy life."

"James, we are brothers now."

"It was not like we were never brothers before."

They both hugged each other and started crying.

"Thank you, dad."

"See you next
summer, Maya!" said
the two of them

James left and
carried on living a
happy life with his
new family or that is
what he thinks.

Thank you to all those
who bought this book.

More books are to come

Other books by this author:

The Adventures of James and The Undying Necklace | First Edition Published: 13th of June 2020

www.ingramcontent.com/pod-product-compliance
Lightning Source LLC
Chambersburg PA
CBHW021015160726
47994CB00006B/2526